THE UNEXPURGATED ADVENTURES OF SHERLOCK HOLMES

BOOK 8

THE SPECKLED BAND SPECULATION

by NP Sercombe

The un-edited manuscript originally entitled *The Adventure of the Speckled Band* written by Dr. John Watson and Sir Arthur Conan Doyle

Illustrations by Emily Snape

This novel is entirely a work of fiction. The names, characters and incidents portrayed in it are the work of the author's and illustrator's imaginations. Any resemblance to actual persons, living or dead, events or localities, is entirely coincidental.

Published by EVA BOOKS 2020 – c/o Harry King Films Limited
1&2 The Barn
West Stoke Road
Lavant
n/r Chichester
West Sussex PO18 9AA

Copyright © NP Sercombe 2020

The rights of Nicholas Sercombe to be identified as the author of this work have been asserted in accordance with the Copyright, Designs and Patents Act 1988.

A CIP catalogue record for this book is available from the British Library.

ISBN 978-1-9996961-7-7 (Hardback)

Book layout & cover design by Clare Brayshaw.

Cover illustration by Emily Snape.

Set in Bruce Old Style.

Prepared and printed by: York Publishing Services Ltd
64 Hallfield Road, Layerthorpe, York YO31 7ZQ

Tel: 01904 431213

Website: www.yps-publishing.co.uk

All rights reserved. No part of this publication may be reproduced, stored in a retrieval system, or transmitted, in any form or by any means; by that we mean electrical, mechanical, photocopying, recording or otherwise, without the prior written permission of the publisher.

This book is sold subject to the condition that it shall not, by way of trade or otherwise, be lent, re-sold, hired out or otherwise circulated without the publisher's prior written consent in any form of binding or cover other than that in which it is published and without similar condition including this condition being imposed on the subsequent purchaser.

THE UNEXPURGATED ADVENTURES OF SHERLOCK HOLMES

Books in the Series:

A BALLS-UP IN BOHEMIA
THE MYSTERIOUS CASE OF MR. GINGERNUTS
THE CASE OF THE RANDY STEPFATHER
MY FIRST PROPER RURAL MURDER
THE ORANGES OF DEATH!
THE MAN WITH THE HAIRY FACE
A GANDER AT THE BLUE CARBUNCLE
THE SPECKLED BAND SPECULATION

Nicholas Sercombe is a writer and producer for film and television. He has been lucky enough to work in comedy for most of the Holocene period with some of the greatest performers and writers. He is most comfortable when reading Conan Doyle and even happier when re-writing these extraordinarily entertaining stories by Dr. John Watson.

Emily Snape is a coffee addicted, London based illustrator, who's work can be found internationally in books, magazines, on the web, television and even buses.

She studied at Central Saint Martins, Bristol and Kingston and is rarely found without a pencil in her hand. She loves sketching in the streets of London and thinks life is too short for matching socks.

For lovers of things that go bump in the night.

The Speckled Band Speculation

(published in The Strand in February 1892 as
THE ADVENTURE OF THE SPECKLED BAND
by Dr. Watson and Arthur Conan Doyle

In glancing over my notes of the cases in which I have during the last few years studied the methods of my friend Sherlock Holmes, I find many tragic, some comic, a large number merely strange, but none commonplace; for, working as he did rather for the love of his art rather than for the acquirement of wealth, he refused to associate himself with any investigation which did not tend towards the unusual, and even the fantastic. Somebody had to look after his finances and his subsistence, and so I had become his business manager to charge for his professional services and Mrs. Hudson a surrogate mother to feed him. Otherwise, even this exceptional human being would have been homeless, emaciated, and, maybe, even dead. We were the life-support *équipe* in the Court of Sherlock Holmes, not that he ever made any effort to show his appreciation; he seized any opportunity he could to confirm his superiority and to admonish us for being his inferiors.

It was early in April, in the year 1890, that I arrived back at 221B Baker Street after a morning of patient consultations. My nephew, William, had spent his last day as my practice secretary and I had taken him to luncheon at The Hereford Arms in the Gloucester Road by way of thanks and a fond farewell. He had made a reasonable job of running my practice, even recruiting some new clients who were not war-torn army veterans with terrible opiate-dependencies*, but after the recent death of his mother, to be frank, dear reader, I was pleased to see him go.

William was released from the Herculean task of attending to his sick parent, with no help from his estranged siblings, and now he needed a proper job. In fact, he needed a career. I had sown the seed of an idea to him to join one of the armed forces and it had taken root in the fertile ground of his young mind. He had plumped for the Navy and was off to Dartmouth the next morning – the Senior Service could look after him instead of me and this was a welcome relief. After all, William was an unexpected responsibility that had been landed on my lap a year or so ago; not that he was a burden, it had suited me well at the time, but now my daily agenda had changed. I spent less time with my patients in my Queensbury Place consulting rooms and I did not have the time to mentor him in training as my replacement. Nor did I have the inclination, because I spent most of my time enjoying the thrill of meeting the weird and wonderful clients as each new case was put in front of the great detective. I was fulfilling many roles. I was his accomplice; his sounding board; his business manager and, most importantly of all, I was the author and illustrator of the accounts of our adventures together. Those accounts were becoming very popular amongst the hoi-polloi, boosting sales of

---

* see *The Case of the Randy Stepfather*

The Strand magazine to five hundred thousand per issue since the owner had drawn up a new contract with me. I was earning more money as a writer in three months than in twelve as a doctor. But, most importantly, I did not share the writing process with Sherlock Holmes. I was free to recount our adventures together precisely as I saw them. Once completed, their only predator in the world was the red pen of *The Strand*'s notorious owner, editor and butcher of my copy, Mr. George Newnes.

It was about four o'clock in the afternoon when I walked into the apartment. All I could hear at the entrance was the loud voices and laughter of another luncheon party. I dumped my medical bag in its place on the French half-moon table, missed the hat stand completely – my own luncheon had been very well-fuelled – retrieved my hat, fixed it in position upon its peg, and ambled into the room itself. Sitting at the head of the dining table was the undomesticated charge who had become the epicentre of my new career.

'If your name was John Harrison,' said Sherlock Holmes, 'instead of John Watson, your timing could not be better, for we have just finished pudding. Draw up a chair, dear Doctor. We are receiving guests.'

His father, Professor Julian, was seated upon his right, nearest to me, and his mother, Wendy, was opposite, so huge and fleshy that she took up the space on the far side of the table. Naturally, she was seated in the Mummy Chair. Both parents smiled warmly as they greeted me. But it was the far end the Regency mahogany that interested me the most, where the beautiful and charismatic Rachel was in the process of coming to my rescue. She was like a valiant knight in battle, rising from the saddle and proclaiming: "God for Harry, England and St. George!" But in reality, she jumped up from her chair and shouted:

'Sherlock! For goodness sakes, why do you have to be so ridiculously pompous?' She pointed her finger at me. 'John is not an occasional friend, just strolled in off the street. He lives with you, here, in this apartment!'

'He does?' quipped Holmes with a provocative smile, which exasperated his sister and earned him a roll of the eyes from his mother, Wendy.

'Take no notice of him, boyo!' said Professor Julian, rising up from his seat and moving his chair to make room for mine, which I positioned between him and his daughter, much closer to her than to him. In fact, deliberately close to her. Professor Julian shook my hand effusively.

'Welcome, boyo! Welcome to our very own luncheon party.'

'Oh, yes, I remember him now...'

'Sherlock!'

'Here, boy, have my glass and refresh yourself.' The Professor pushed one of his wine glasses in front of me and poured a healthy serving from the decanter. 'This is something very special that Wendy and I brought along with us today, all the way from Godalming: a very, very fine Welsh claret.'

'Daddy! Stop teasing. Take no notice, John. The wine is Chateau Lagrange.'

'Very, very good for you, boyo,' recommended the esteemed physicist, and handed the glass to me. 'I am on the sweet stuff,' said he, and I noticed that he was on the pudding wine, 'which is ab-so-lute-ly delicious.

It is giving my teeth a thoroughly good clean! Tidy!' And he chinked glasses with me.

'I hear that your nephew, William, has secured himself a commission in the Royal Navy,' remarked Holmes.

'Yes, Holmes he has a commission. I am immensely proud of him.'

Rachel sighed dreamily. 'A life on the ocean wave,' she whispered seductively, with her arm on the table, her chin cupped in her palm and her eyes lost in the clouds. 'How romantic!'

'More like a life of rum, bum and baccy, my girl!'

'Oh, Daddy!' said Rachel, giving me a minty wink of her emerald eye. 'How could you tease John so?'

Infused by wine and enthused by banter the party continued. Mrs. Hudson made an appearance with a doorstop of cheddar and a truckle of stilton, in my humble opinion the only two cheeses worth introducing to any educated palate. Holmes was as relaxed as I had ever seen him, drinking port and smoking cigarettes, his favourites: Sullivan Powell No.2s. Julian was just as energetic as the first time I met him; always laughing, gesticulating, waving his arms around, shouting "Tidy!" and pulling everyone's legs until they came off, with Rachel berating her father theatrically for every portion of silliness, and then flicking her eyes at me to measure my reaction. Hmm! She was flirting. Well, if she was walking back into my life I would make sure that the pathway was clear. I found her very attractive and became entwined in her spell, laughing more carelessly at each one of her gibes. Wendy just soaked up the ambience through her wrinkled face;

always quiet, probably still suffering sciatica, but she noticed our chemistry. I was thoroughly enjoying myself until, suddenly, everyone went quiet. Holmes rose from his seat and fetched a leather case. He placed it carefully upon the mat in front of him. Even before he had opened it up, the family burst into sympathetic applause but I was thrown into a state of panic as I registered the shape. Holmes opened Pandora's Box, eyes sparkling, to greet his violin. My jaw dropped onto the table. A bloody violin! I am not a stringed instrument man – I despised any doodad that involved someone sawing it in half to obtain a sound, the exception being the Spanish guitar which was just a matter of nimble fingers and a bandana.

'Ahhh, it is good to see you, Horatio, my old friend!' he cooed, and lifted the instrument up to his lips, planting a smacker upon his tailpiece, right next to his F-hole. 'We have been estranged too long.'

"Horatio" was a violin of typically dark chestnut hue. His ancient varnish reflected the wavering candlelight with a warm, romantic diffusion. Much as I despised his very existence my eye was caught by his shape: his elegant lines, harmonious curves and scrolls, the pure purfling and bridge, which, when combined, were a work of art. But my admiration delayed my dive for the door and a hasty exit – a nasty consequence – because without further ado, Holmes tucked Horatio under his chin and wielded the bow. It was obvious that he had a talent for the instrument but a cacophonous discord seared the air, like a rookery being attacked by a flock of swifts, a hundred voices screaming all at once! I looked around the table. Dad, Mum and horny daughter were all gripped by the same fear as me: eyes staring into a void; faces set in stone; bodies rigid and lifeless. Luckily, Holmes had a fine musical ear, and despite his love for this old friend, he stopped playing. He set Horatio down on the table.

'He needs some tender loving care,' said Holmes.

'He needs some tender loving tuning!' said I.

Holmes nodded his head in what he imagined to be our mutual appreciation of the violin. He smiled and glanced at me. Dammit! I had said the wrong thing!

'Indeed, Doctor, I forgot. The fact that you have a fine musical ear is not in doubt. You have accompanied me to a virtuoso recital.' Then, Holmes waxed lyrical to his family about our adventure in the City a little while ago,* even showing a tinge of emotion, a tear in his eye. 'Why, the good doctor and I were fortunate enough to catch the sublime Pablo de Sarasate, at the St. James's Hall.'

'By climbing through the loo window,' said I.

'That's a strange way to get in, boyo?'

'We had spent all of our money on luncheon.'

'Tidy!'

'You, me and Horatio,' said Holmes, 'have many enjoyable nights ahead of us.'

I did not reply. I could not reply! I had no idea whether my friend was a poor player – he had looked as if he had a modicum of talent, that was for sure – but it was the sound of the instrument itself that finished me off. Now I would have to live with it. Maybe Holmes would treat it like the chap who knows how to play the bagpipes but, because he is a *gentleman*, he chooses

---

* see *The Mysterious Case of Mr. Gingernuts*

I didn't need to be a doctor to diagnose Professor Julian 100% tone-deaf

not to? No, Holmes wouldn't do that! I heaved myself up and ambled over to the sideboard, wondering how I could hijack the heinous instrument. Whilst the family chattered about the triumph of Horatio being restored to his rightful owner – sub-text: the benefits of removing Horatio from their lives by delivering it here – I poured myself an obscene dollop of brandy. One, doleful swig later, found me musing over the graceful lines of Rachel's exquisite beauty instead of the seductive lines of a violin. She laughed at one of her father's silly jokes – it may have been the one about them all staying in my room for the night, ha, ha, – and her face lit up all summery, the curves of her elegant figure moving symphonically. My deep appreciation caused a dramatic stirring in the trouser department! I had to make my move but then I remembered the terrible rift of last year, when Holmes imagined that I had been rogering his sister (and I wasn't).* I could not, and would not, risk a revival of the same quarrel, losing a dear friend *and* such a rich source of income. No! I stopped myself short and pondered a while. Hmmm! I looked at her again. My lust took over! If Holmes had his playmate, Horatio, then I would have mine too, but this time the courtship would have to be much more subtle. I went and sat down next to Rachel... and pulled my chair even closer.

* * *

I awoke the next morning to find Sherlock Holmes standing, fully dressed, by the side of my bed. He was a later riser as a rule, and, as the clock on the mantelpiece showed me that it was only a quarter past seven, I

---

* see *My First Proper Rural Murder*

blinked up at him in some surprise, and perhaps just a little resentment, for I was myself a regular in my habits.

'Very sorry to knock you up, Watson,' said he, 'but it's the common lot this morning. Mrs. Hudson has been knocked up, she retorted upon me, and I on you.' Then, strangely, he flicked his eyes around the room.

'What is it then? A fire?'

'No, a client,' said he, now changing his position, hopping from one foot to the other, and peering at my bed from different angles. 'It seems that a young lady has arrived in a considerable state of excitement, who insists upon seeing me. She is waiting now in the sitting room. Now, when young ladies wander about the metropolis at this hour of the morning, and knock sleepy people up out of their beds, I presume that is something very pressing which they have to communicate. Should it prove to be an interesting case, you would, I am sure, wish to follow it from the outset. I thought at any rate that I should call you, and give you a chance.'

Pants on fire! He was checking to see whether Rachel was in the room with me, and I decided to do something about it.

'My dear fellow, I would not miss it for anything. But hold on, my friend, you seem to be searching for something? Oh, I know...' Then, I lifted the bedsheets and hollered under: 'I may be a while, Rachel dear, but I won't be long, do you hear?'

'Oh, ha, ha, Watson. I happen to know that my sister is fast asleep at The Goring, a mile away from your despicable clutches. I heard something during the night that may have come from this direction, that is all.' He delivered his snub with brusqueness before studying me for a moment and then breaking into a smile. 'My, you are looking peaky, Doctor. I must say, you did punish the cognac. Ha! You will be suffering from its overnight metamorphosis from ethanol to ethanoic acid. But come along now, show a leg! I have a feeling in my bones that this lady has a fantastic story to tell us.' He departed the room, with a spring in his step.

How could I forget that he was a Doctor of Chemistry? I jumped out of bed and started to throw on my clothes. Suddenly I felt dizzy and stopped. My head was swimming. My stomach was churning. My mouth was dry. How much had I had to drink yesterday? I made a quick calculation and groaned. My diagnosis: a dire hangover. My prognosis: a painful morning ahead.

Just off, in the sitting room, I could hear: 'Good morning, madam. My name is Sherlock Holmes...' And then his voice burbled along in the background as I made myself ready. A few minutes later I followed in my friend's footsteps along from the front door to the sitting room. I had no keener pleasure than in joining Holmes in his professional investigations, and in admiring the rapid deductions, as swift as intuitions, and yet always found on a logical basis, with which he unravelled the problems which were submitted to him. A lady dressed in black and heavily veiled, who had been sitting in the window, looked up as I entered.

'This is my intimate friend and associate, Dr. Watson, before whom you can speak as freely as before myself. Do not worry about his appearance – he always looks like that.' He threw me a mischievous grin. 'Ha!

I am glad to see that Mrs. Hudson has had the good sense to light the fire. These Spring mornings often have a chill about them and today is no exception. Pray, draw up to it, whilst we wait for our housekeeper to bring us a cup of hot coffee, for I observe that you are shivering.

'It is not the cold that which makes me shiver,' said the woman in a low voice, changing her seat as requested.

'What, then?' said Holmes, his voice dropping to a more sombre tone whilst he sat himself down in a chair next to her.

'It is fear, Mr. Holmes. It is terror.' She raised her veil as she spoke and immediately I felt sorry for the poor woman – she looked worse than I felt! I would say that she was about thirty, but her hair was shot with premature grey, and any youthful beauty was lost in her expression, which was weary and haggard. We could see that she was indeed in a pitiable state of agitation, her face all drawn and grey, with restless, frightened eyes, like those of some hunted animal. I placed my chair next to the great detective and leaned in close. Holmes pulled away and glared at me a moment – I think it was my hangover dragon-breath that startled him – before turning back to the lady. Sherlock Holmes ran over her with one of his quick, all-comprehensive glances before pouring on some charming reassurance. I must say, he had a splendid bedside manner.

'You must not fear,' said he soothingly, bending forward and patting her forearm. 'We shall soon set matters right, I have no doubt. You have come in by train this morning, I see.'

'You must know me then?'

'No, I observe the second half of a return ticket in the palm of your left glove. You must have started early, and yet you had a good drive in a dog-cart, along heavy roads, before you reached the railway station.'

The lady gave a violent start and stared in bewilderment at my companion.

'There is no mystery, my dear madam,' said he, smiling. 'The left arm of your jacket is splattered with mud in no less than seven places. The marks are perfectly fresh.. there is no vehicle save a dog-cart which throws up mud in that way, and then, only when you sit on the left-hand side of the driver.

'Whatever your reasons may be, you are perfectly correct,' said she. 'I started from home before six, reached Leatherhead at twenty past and came in by the first train to Waterloo. Sir, I can stand this strain no longer, I shall go mad if it continues. I have no one to turn to – none, save the only one, who cares for me, and he, poor fellow, can be of little aid. I have heard of you, Mr. Holmes; I have heard of you from Mrs. Byrdd-Flue, whom you helped in the hour of her sore need. It was from her that I had your address. Oh, sir, do you not think you could help me too, and at least throw a little light through the dense darkness which surrounds me? At present it is out of my power to reward you for your services.'

Not another pauper for a client!

'But in a month or two I shall be married, with the control of my own income, and then at least you shall not find me ungrateful.'

Hopeful...

Holmes turned to his desk, and, unlocking it, drew out a small casebook which he consulted.

'Byrdd-Flue,' said he. 'Ah, yes, I recall the case; it was concerned with an opal tiara. I think it was before your time, Watson. I can only say, madam, that I shall be happy to devote the same care to your case as I did to that of your friend. As to reward, my profession is its own reward...'

'May I just butt in here?' said I, mustering all of my remaining strength.

'No.'

'Madam,' I croaked, 'it is I who tends to the administrative matters in the great detective's consultations.'

'Shut up, Watson!' said Holmes excitedly, pulling up his chair away from me and closer to our visitor whilst indicating that I should stay where I was. Did I smell that bad? Hmmm, probably.

'And now, madam,' oozed Holmes soothingly, 'I beg that you will lay before us everything that may help us in forming an opinion upon the matter.'

As our new client started to tell her story I looked around to see Mrs. Hudson entering the room. She was carrying a tray of hot, aromatic treats. Just as she passed by my bedroom, I could see the door twitch and some long, slender fingers clasp the architrave. My goodness, was Rachel ready to make her escape?

'Ah, Mrs. Hudson!' I exclaimed, jumping up out of my seat, which was when a searing pain shot up my leg, through my groin and arrived at my vocal cords.

'The Jezail bullet!' I screamed. Then I collapsed into the fireplace.

My audition for the Marylebone Amateur Dramatic Society was a triumph!

Sherlock Holmes did not like to be interrupted during a client interview, especially when the lady had only just started to tell us her story, but he rose from his seat with a sigh. He came to my rescue with a "he was in the wars, this one" to the lady visitor as he picked me up and placed me back into my chair. Mrs. Hudson served the coffee, hot buttery toast and muffins, carrying on as if nothing had happened.

'Will that be all, gentlemen?' said she, her voice laden with sarcasm, dropping an insolent curtsy.

'Thank you, Mrs. Hudson. Now, off you go,' said Sherlock Holmes. He was tuned-in to her ironical insolence but Mrs. Hudson simply ignored his curt dismissal. But she gave me a smile that said it all; a knowing smile that told me that she had seen Rachel, knew that my Jezail bullet attack was a distraction for Sherlock Holmes and that now this new secret was her new blackmail. From that moment on, I knew that our landlady would require payment for her discretion, and we knew what that entailed, didn't we dear loyal adventure-enthusiast? Oh, it never rains but it pours!

Once we had settled down, with our occasional tables laden, the great detective sighed. 'Have you quite finished fooling around, Doctor? May this lady begin?'

'The bullet has moved back from the nerve again now, thank you, Holmes. Please excuse my old war wound, madam, and reveal your story to us.'

'My name is Sharon Stoner. I have heard, Mr. Holmes, that you can see deeply into the manifold wickedness of the human heart. You may advise me how to walk amid the dangers which encompass me.'

'I am all attention, Miss Stoner.'

'I am living with my stepfather, who is the last survivor of one of the oldest Saxon families in England, the Boycotts of Stoke Moran, on the western border of Surrey, near Leatherhead.'

Holmes nodded his head. 'The name is familiar to me,' said he. They are neighbours of the Hudsons, the celebrated financier married to the soap magnate.'

'The same, Mr. Holmes. The Boycott family was, at one time, among the richest in England, and the estate extended over the borders into Berkshire in the north, and Hampshire in the west. In the last century, however, four successive heirs were of dissolute and wasteful disposition, and the family ruin was eventually completed by a gambler, in the days of the Regency. Nothing was left save a few acres of ground and the two-hundred-year-old house, which is itself crushed under a heavy mortgage. The last squire dragged out his existence there, living the horrible life of an aristocratic pauper; but his only son, my stepfather, seeing that he must adapt himself to the new conditions, obtained an advance from a relative, which enabled him to take a medical degree, and went out to Calcutta, where, by his professional skill and his force of character, he established a large practice. In a fit of anger, however, caused by some robberies which had been perpetrated in the house, he beat his native butler to death, and narrowly escaped a capital sentence. As it was, he suffered a long term of imprisonment, and afterwards returned to England a morose and disappointed man.

'When Dr. Boycott was in India he married my mother, Mrs. Honey Stoner, the young widow of Major-General Stoner, of the Bengal Artillery. My sister Sandra and I were twins, and we were only two years old at the time of my mother's re-marriage.'

So, Sharon Stoner had a mother, Honey Stoner, and a sister called Sandy Stoner. What were the odds, I wondered, on her grandmother being called Pumice?

'My mother had a considerable sum of money, not less than a thousand a year, and this she bequeathed to Dr. Boycott entirely whilst we resided with him, with a provision that a certain annual sum should be allowed to each of us in the event of our marriage. Shortly after our return to England my mother died – she was killed eight years ago in a railway accident near Crewe. Dr. Boycott then abandoned his attempts to establish himself in practice in London and took us to live with him in the ancestral home at Stoke Moran. The money which my mother had left was enough for all our wants and there seemed no obstacle to our happiness.

'But a terrible change came over our stepfather about this time. Instead of making fresh friends and exchanging visits with our neighbours, who had at first been overjoyed to see a Boycott of Stoke Moran back in the old family seat, he shut himself up in his house, and seldom came out, save to indulge in ferocious quarrels with whoever might cross his path. A violence of temper that was approaching mania has been hereditary in the men of the family, and in my stepfather's case it had, I believe, been intensified by his long residence in the tropics. A series of disgraceful brawls took place, two of which ended in the police-court, until at last be became the terror of the village, and the folks would fly at his approach, for he is man of immense strength, and absolutely uncontrollable in his anger.

'Last week he hurled the local blacksmith over a parapet into a stream and it was only by paying over all the money that I could gather together that I was able to avert another public exposure. He had no friends at all save the wandering gipsies, and he would give these vagabonds leave to encamp upon the few acres of bramble-covered land which represents the family estate and would accept in return the hospitality of their tents, wandering away with them sometimes for weeks on end. He has a passion also for Indian animals, which are sent over to him by a correspondent, and he has at this moment a cheetah and a baboon, which wander freely over his grounds, and are feared by the villagers almost as much as their master.

'You can imagine from what I say that my poor sister Sandra and I had no great pleasure in our lives. No servant would stay with us, and for a long time we did all the work in the house. She was but thirty at the time of her death, and yet her hair had already begun to whiten, even as mine has.'

'Your sister is dead, then?'

'She died just two years ago, and it is of her death that I wish to speak to you.'

Death? Goodness me, *I* was about to die! From my hangover, from Holmes's so-called "ethanoic acid" poisoning. I slunk down in my chair and tried to think my way out of my living hell.

'You can understand that, living the life which I have described, we were unlikely to see any one of our own age and position. We had, however, an aunt, my mother's maiden sister, Miss Honoria Westphail, who lives near Harrow, and we were occasionally allowed to pay short visits at this lady's house. Sandra went there at Christmas two years ago, and met there a half-pay Major of Marines, to whom she became engaged. My stepfather learned of the engagement when my sister returned and offered no objection to the marriage; but within a fortnight of the day which had been fixed for the wedding, the terrible event occurred which has deprived me of my only companion.'

She paused for breath, thank goodness, her voice being rather monotonous and wavering. I filled my lungs and checked my heart was still beating. Sherlock Holmes had been leaning back in his chair with his eyes closed, and his head sunk in a cushion but I knew that he was taking in every vowel and consonant. He half opened his lids now and glanced across at Miss Sharon Stoner.

'Pray, be precise as to details,' said he. His words sounded slightly distant as my hangover tightened its grip. I sank into the warm fire, *my* lids now getting heavy...

'It is easy for me to be so, for every event of that dreadful time is seared into my memory. The manor house is, as I have already said, very old, and only one wing is now inhabited. The bedrooms in this wing are on the ground floor; the sitting-rooms being in the central block of the buildings. Of these bedrooms, the first is Dr. Boycott's, the second my sister's, and the third my own.'

And no doubt the fourth belongs to the baboon? After yesterday's lunch and last night's activities I was feeling weary, and not receptive to so much detail. I kept my peace, however, because the mood was dominated by the vulnerable figure of Sharon Stoner, all-a-tremble.

'There is no communication between them, but they all open out into the same corridor. Do I make myself plain?'

'Perfectly so,' said Holmes sternly, then nudging me with his elbow and breaking my slumber. 'WOULDN'T YOU AGREE, DOCTOR!' he barked. I nodded agreement, pinching my right ear lobe to wake myself up. This didn't seem to bother Sharon Stoner, though, who continued, unabated.

'The windows of the three rooms open out upon the lawn. That fatal night Dr. Boycott had gone to his room early, though we knew that he had not retired to rest, for my sister was troubled by the smell of strong Indian cigars which it was his custom to smoke.'

But maybe the baboon enjoys a post-prandial cheroot or two?

'Sandra left her room and came into mine, where she sat for some time, chatting about her approaching wedding. At eleven o'clock she rose to leave me, but she paused at the door and looked back.

'"Tell me, my dear Sharona," said she, "have you ever heard anyone whistle in the dead of the night?"'

Sharona! Holmes and I stole a glance and muffled our guffaws at the silliness of our client's pet name. But we were too polite to interrupt Miss Sharona, who was blissfully unaware of our cynicism.

'"Never,"' said I.

'"I suppose that you could not possibly whistle to yourself in your sleep?"'

'"Certainly not! But why do you ask?"'

'"Because during the last few nights I have always, about three in the morning, heard a low clear whistle. I am a light sleeper, and it has awakened me. I cannot tell where it came from – perhaps from the next room, perhaps from the lawn. I thought that I would just ask you whether you had heard it."'

'"No, I have not. It must be those wretched gipsies in the plantation."'

'"Very likely. And yet if it were on the lawn I wonder that you did not hear it also."'

'"Ah, but I sleep more heavily than you."'

'"Well, it is of no great consequence, at any rate."' She smiled back at me, closed my door, and a few moments later I heard her key turn in the lock.'

'Indeed,' said Holmes. 'Was it your custom always to lock yourselves in at night?'

'Always.'

'And, why?'

'I think that I mentioned to you that the Doctor kept a cheetah and a baboon. We had no feeling of security unless our doors were always locked.'

I was fading again, feeling tired and, now, quite nauseous. I experienced a reflux but managed to swallow hard and control it. I gave my lobe another pinch and pushed myself up in my chair. Holmes was staring at me.

'For goodness sakes, take some more coffee, Doctor,' said he. He flicked his eyes back to Sharona Stoner (I suppose it rhymed very well)? 'Please excuse my fatigued associate. He has been overdoing things recently. Pray, proceed with your statement.'

'Thank you, Mr. Holmes,' sighed she, going flush in the cheek and getting short of breath. 'But do not concern yourself about your companion. You may have to please bear with me for I shall struggle to tell you the climax of this story in such good heart, such is my strong emotional attachment I have to recent events.' She dropped her face into her hands and sobbed.

'Dr. Watson – can you please assist, Miss Stoner?'

I rose unsteadily from my seat and stood next to our visitor. I took her pulse by holding her wrist with one hand and placed the palm of my other onto the small of her back, rubbing gently. 'Take some air, Miss Stoner,' I mumbled, trying desperately not to be sick.

She drew in some deep breaths, held them for a moment, and then let them out.

'In, out,' I commanded. 'In, out. In, out.' Oh my God I was feeling ill...

My eyes dipped down. She had stopped crying and was lifting her bosoms nicely, which were remarkably plump, and then letting them down again. Up, down. Up, down. Mmmm! Her poor face may have been filled with angst but her youthful figure was *quite* remarkable! I began to feel a little better. Holmes caught my peripheral as he rolled his eyes heavenwards.

'Fixing one's gaze on the horizon is a well-known cure for sea-sickness, is it not, Doctor?'

What was he talking about? Oh! Suddenly I realised my mesmerisation with Sharon Stoner's top hamper and stood back, embarrassed. 'Indeed, Holmes, indeed... Are you feeling better, Miss Stoner?'

'Yes, thank you, Dr. Watson. I shall continue with my story.'

I wobbled a path back to my seat and composed myself into a carefully selected position, one in which I was least likely to vomit over our new client. Holmes and I prepared ourselves for an emotional revelation, somewhat nervously. As it turned out, no amount of prep could have prepared Holmes and I for the next instalment of the story, hangover or not.

'I could not sleep that night,' she said, with determined resolve in her voice. 'A vague feeling of impending misfortune impressed me. My sister and I, you will recollect, were twins, and you know how subtle are the links which bind two souls who are so closely allied. It was a wild night. The wind was howling outside, and the rain was beating and splashing against the windows. Suddenly, amidst all the hubbub of the gale, there burst forth the wild scream of a terrified woman. I knew that it was my sister's voice. I sprang from my bed, wrapped a shawl around me, and rushed into the corridor. As I opened my door I seemed to hear a low whistle, such as my sister described, and a few moments later a clanging sound, as if a mass of metal had fallen. As I ran down the passage my sister's door was unlocked and revolved slowly upon its hinges. I stared at it horror-stricken, not knowing what was about to issue from it. By the light of the corridor lamp I saw my sister appear at the opening, her face blanched with terror, her hands groping for help, her whole figure swaying to and fro, like that of a drunkard. I ran to her, but at that moment her knees seemed to give way and she fell to the ground. She writhed as one who is in terrible pain, and her limbs were dreadfully convulsed. At first I thought that she had not recognised me, but as I bent over her she suddenly shrieked out in a voice which I shall never forget, "Oh, my God! Sharon! It was the band! The speckled band!" There was something else which she would fain have said, and she stabbed her finger into the air in the direction of the Doctor's room, but a fresh convulsion seized her and choked her words. I rushed out, calling loudly for my stepfather, and I met him hastening from his room in his dressing-gown. When he reached my sister's side she was unconscious, and though he poured brandy down her throat, and sent for medical aid from the village, all efforts were in vain, for she slowly sank and died without having recovered her consciousness. Such was the dreadful end of my beloved sister, Sandra.'

'One moment,' said Holmes; 'are you sure about this whistle and metallic sound? Could you swear to it?'

'That was what the county coroner asked me at the inquiry. It is my strong impression that I heard it, and yet among the crash of the gale, and the creaking of an old house, I may possibly have been deceived.'

'Was your sister dressed?'

'No, she was in her nightdress. In her right hand was found a charred stump of a match, and in her left a matchbox.'

Showing that she had struck a light and looked about her when the alarm took place. That is important. And what conclusion did the coroner come to?'

'He investigated the case with great care, for Dr. Boycott's conduct had long been notorious in the county, but he was unable to find any satisfactory cause of death. My evidence showed that the door had been fastened upon the inner side, and the windows were blocked by old-fashioned shutters with broad iron bars, which were secured every night. The walls were carefully sounded, and were shown to be quite solid all round, and the flooring was also thoroughly examined, with the same result. The chimney brake is wide but is barred up by four large staples. It is certain, therefore, that my sister was quite alone when she met her end. Besides, there were no marks of any violence upon her.'

'How about poison?'

'The doctors examined her for it, but without success.'

'What do you think that this unfortunate lady died of, then?'

It is my belief that she died of pure fear and nervous shock, though what it was which frightened her I cannot imagine.'

'Were the gipsies in the plantation at the time?'

'Yes, there are nearly always some there.'

'Ah, and what did you gather from this allusion to a band – a speckled band?'

'Sometimes I have thought that it was merely the wild talk of delirium, sometimes that it may have referred to some band of people, perhaps to these very gipsies in the plantation. I do not know whether the spotted handkerchiefs which so many of them wear over their heads might have suggested the strange adjective which she used.'

Holmes shook his head like a man who is far from being satisfied. He pressed his long slender fingers together into a steeple and rested his head upon its roof. He flashed his eyes over to me, creasing, then flinty, at the sight of me bewitched by a rhythmic hammer striking an anvil on the inside of my cranium. Thud! Thud! Thud!

'These are very deep waters,' said he. 'And the good Doctor here is playing host to Hephaestus.'

How did he know? How *could* he know about the cranial hammering!

'Pray, go on with your narrative,' said he to Sharon Stoner.

There was more? My goodness, I was feeling awfully shaky, and I was sweating like a Derby winner. Even Miss Stoner was giving me worried glances. I needed to get out of the conference, to find some sort of tincture to cure myself; even a pint of water could be vital.

'Two years have passed since then...'

There *was* more!

'My life has been until lately lonelier than ever. A month ago, however, a dear friend, whom I have known for many years, has done me the honour to ask for my hand in marriage. His name is Armitage – Percy Armitage – the second son of Mr. Armitage, of Crane Water, near Reading. My stepfather has offered no opposition to the match, and we are to be married in the course of the Spring. Two days ago, some repairs were started in the west wing of the building, and my bedroom wall has been pierced, so that I have had to move into the chamber in which my sister died, and to sleep in the very bed in which she slept.'

Sharon Stoner paused. She was getting herself into a froth again and she started to tremble, the pitch of her voice wavering up and down, the poor creature. I watched the great detective. He was totally enraptured by this case; his eyes open wider, forcing his lids into a bulge, just like a pet goldfish.

'Imagine, then,' she twittered, 'my thrill of terror when last night, as I lay awake, thinking over her terrible fate, I suddenly heard in the silence of the night the low whistle which had been the herald of her own death. I sprang up and lit the lamp, but nothing was to be seen in the room. I was too shaken to go to bed again, however, so I dressed, and as soon as it was daylight I slipped down, got a dog-cart at the Crown Inn, which is opposite, and drove to Leatherhead, from whence I have come this morning, with the one object of seeing you and asking your advice.'

'You have done wisely,' said my friend. 'But have you told me all?'

'Yes, all.'

'Miss Stoner, you have not told me all. You are screening your stepfather.'

'Why, what do you mean?'

For answer Holmes pushed back the frill of black lace which fringed the hand that lay upon our visitor's knee. Five little livid spots, the marks of four fingers and a thumb, were printed upon the white wrist. Hmmm. They looked nasty!

'You have been cruelly used,' said Holmes.

The lady coloured deeply and covered her injured wrist. 'He is a hard man,' she said, 'and perhaps he hardly knows his own strength.'

There was a long silence, during which Holmes leaned his chin upon his hands and stared into the crackling fire.

This is a very deep business,' he said at last. 'There are a thousand details which I should desire to know before I decide upon the course of action. Yet we have not a moment to lose. If we were to come to Stoke Moran today, would it be possible for us to see over these rooms without the knowledge of your stepfather?'

'As it happens, he spoke of coming into town today upon some most important business. It is probable that he will be away all day, and that there would be nothing to disturb you. We have a housekeeper now, but she is old and foolish, and I could easily get her out of the way.'

'Excellent. You are not averse to this trip, Watson?'

I felt dreadful, like I had been run over by a four-wheeler full of fat people, but this was one of the most intriguing collection of occurrences that I had heard, even when keeping the company of Sherlock Holmes. We were about to embark upon a most fascinating mystery, which was an odds-on certainty to make a till-busting story for Newnes at *The Strand*. I had to pull myself together.

'By all means!' I chirruped. "But please, please, please could we have some breakfast first, before we depart?'

'By no means, Watson. The game's afoot!'

'Actually, Mr. Holmes...' said this wonderful, sympathetic lady, mewing at my appearance, the sweat now running down my glaucous temples onto my shirt collar. 'Actually, I have one or two things which I wish to do now that I am in town. But I shall return by the 12 o'clock train, so as to be there in time for your coming.'

'Then we shall wait and breakfast. Will you join us?

'No, I must go. My heart is lightened already since I have confided my trouble to you. I shall look forward to seeing you again this afternoon.'

'You may expect us early in the afternoon,' said Holmes.

She dropped her thick black veil over her face and glided from the room.

'And what do you think of it all, Watson?' asked Sherlock Holmes, leaning back in his chair.

'It seems to me to be a most dark and sinister business.'

'Indeed, it is, Watson. Now, how are you feeling?'

'I am dying, Holmes.'

'Good! That will teach you to spend all afternoon slobbering over my sister at the dining table.'

Little did he know that my slobbering over Rachel had extended through the night. He would be the one who was taught a lesson. She may have been escorted from 221B Baker Street by Professor Julian and Wendy, but we had made a plan. That plan had worked. This thought lifted my spirits a little. Hephaestus had downed tools and I was sweating no longer.

'Why, Holmes, would you be so concerned about Rachel and I engaging in perfectly civilised conversation, hmmm?' I rose from my chair more steadily. 'Now, if you don't mind, I must engage in mortal combat with the remains of this hangover. I must drink water, with salts. I must eat victuals, with lashings of fat.'

'What about some drugs?'

'Medicine? Yes, I could use some medicine!'

'Well, you need medicine. I need pleasure. I'll raise a glass to that. Fetch your medicine bag and I shall whistle up Mrs. Hudson for a hearty breakfast.'

* * *

About an hour later we were stuffed with grub. We had taken eggs, kidneys and chops, all washed down with an excellent Indian pale ale. I was washed out but feeling much better. After that, Sherlock Holmes tapped into my medicines, into the bag of bliss, by partaking the purest cocaine that my profession had to offer, which was a treat for him as he was never normally allowed into it. This was one of the amazing things about my companion; that he respected my wishes in this area of my life and, despite his reckless dalliances with some drugs, which he knew that I would have stocked in the bag, he never touched them without my permission. Of course, I had to put a padlock on it for security, but this was only for form's sake because Holmes picked it open within two bats of an eyelid. It was his party trick and I timed him on each occasion. This time – half-hunter at the ready – it had been fourteen seconds, about the same as it took him to submerge a Robin's egg of the pure-stuff into his bloodstream.

'By the way, Holmes there is something I have been meaning to ask you for a while now. Closing up my medical bag has reminded me.'

'What, pray, is on the precipice of your imagination, Watson?'

'How did you learn to unpick the combinations in a lock, such as this padlock here?'

'One word: Teddy.'

'Professor Moriarty!'

'Indeed so, Watson. As a child, James held a fascination for locks and keys. When we were growing up together he had made a study of their mechanics, going way back to when the Egyptians invented the

Holmes caught a whiff of the pure stuff and posted a record-breaking lock-pick.

mortice lock, right up to the notable contemporary inventors, George Davis and Charles Chubb.'

It was a good job that my hangover had abated because nothing was going to stop the cocaine-riddled detective from talking now – he was rattling off the words like a man in confession sailing over a waterfall.

'The mechanics-are-relatively-simple-for-a-man-of-my-intellect-and-it didn't-take-me-long-to-master-most-of-the-so-called-security-devices-but-Teddy-was-always-one-step-ahead-of-me-it-was-he-who-mastered-the-five-and-seven-tumbler-devices-which-are-used-on most-modern-safes.' He paused for breath, then… 'These-are-beyond-my-skills-there-is-nobody-alive-who-knows-more-upon-the-subject-of-locks. He is a genius.'

He had had enough! I locked my medical bag and placed it upon the floor. If it was out of sight, it may be out of mind. He was still prattling on about Professor Moriarty's prowess as a locksmith and I had to stop him somehow. I knew that the only way to achieve that was to bring him back to the mystery in hand, the terrible quandary of Miss Sharon Stoner.

'I say, Holmes, if Miss Stoner is correct in saying that the flooring and walls are sound, and that the door, window and chimney are impassable, then her sister must have been undoubtedly alone when she met her mysterious end.'

'What becomes, then, of these nocturnal whistles? And what of the very peculiar words of a dying woman? And why did the sister refer to our client as "Sharona" when her name is Sharon?'

'I cannot think straight, Holmes,' said I, 'even though my head is clearing and my stomach is settled.'

'When you combine the ideas of whistles at night, the presence of a band of gipsies who are on intimate terms with this old doctor, the fact that we have every reason to believe that the doctor has an interest in preventing his stepdaughter's marriage, the dying allusion to a band, the fact that Miss Sharon Stoner heard a metallic clang, which might have been caused by one of those metal bars which secured the shutters falling back into their place, I think there is good ground to think that the mystery may be cleared along those lines.'

All of that was just one sentence. Do you see now, dear reader, why I tried my best to steer Holmes away from cocaine? But we had to keep going, so next I asked him how did he think that the gipsies fitted into this situation?

'I haven't got a clue,' said he. 'It is precisely for this reason that we are going to Stoke Moran this day. I want to see whether the objections are fatal, or if they may be explained away. But...'

Suddenly, there was a loud crash as the apartment door burst open!

'Who, in the name of the devil is this?' Holmes shouted out loud, his whole frame gone rigid in the ejaculation.

'Goodness knows, Holmes,' said I. 'It's like Piccadilly Circus round here today!' I swivelled around in my seat to gain a view of the door. 'Goodness me, you are a big chap!'

There was a huge man framed in the aperture, and he was wide-eyed fuming! His costume was a peculiar mixture of the professional and of the agricultural, having a black top-hat, a long frock-coat, and a pair of high gaiters, with a hunting-crop swinging in his hand. So tall was he that his hat actually brushed the lintel of the doorway, and his breadth seemed to span it across from side to side. A large face, seared with a thousand wrinkles, burned yellow with the sun, and marked with every evil passion, was turned from one side to the other of us, while his deep-set, bile-shot eyes, and the high, thin, curved nose, gave him somewhat the resemblance to a fierce old bird of prey. Apart from that, dear reader, he was an oil painting!

'Which of you is Holmes?' asked this apparition.

'That is my name, sir, but you have the advantage of me,' said my companion quietly.

'I am Dr. Grimesby Boycott, of Stoke Moran.'

'Indeed, Doctor,' said Holmes blandly. 'Pray, take a seat.'

'I will do nothing of the kind. My stepdaughter has been here. I have traced her. What has she been saying to you?'

'It is a little cold for the time of year,' said Holmes. 'Do you not find it so, Doctor?'

'What has she been saying to you?!' screamed the old man furiously. He took a pace forward into the apartment itself. Now, I was able to catch a glimpse of Mrs. Hudson lurking behind him with a determined look upon her face.

'But I have heard that crocuses promise well,' continued my companion imperturbably.

'Ha! You put me off, do you?' said our new visitor, taking another step forward, and shaking his hunting-crop. Little did he know that our landlady was behind him holding a truncheon. Well, I think it was a truncheon…

'I know you, you scoundrel!' he shouted, 'I have heard of you before. You are Holmes the meddler.'

My friend smiled.

'Holmes the busybody!'

His smile broadened.

'Holmes the Scotland Yard jack-in-the-box smart-arse!

Holmes chuckled heartily. 'Your conversation is most entertaining,' said he. 'When you go out close the door, for there is a dreadful draught in here.'

'I will go when I have had my say! I know that Miss Stoner has been here – I traced her. Don't you dare meddle with my affairs!'

'My dear sir, I have a distinct feeling of *déjà vu*. I have heard this all before, only a few moments ago. Now, get out.'

'Damn your impertinence, sir! I am a dangerous man to fall foul of! See here.' He stepped up to the mantelpiece, directly in front of Holmes, and seized the poker. He held it up, as a demonstration to us all, even Mrs. Hudson – who he had just caught a glimpse of for the first time – and bent it into a curve with his huge brown hands.

'See that you keep yourself out of my grip,' he snarled, and hurled the twisted-now-redundant, poker into the fireplace.

Holmes stood up. He squared up to the Doctor, who sensed an attack and tensed up. Both men were about the same height. They eye-balled each other: the hairy gorilla, in the red corner, was the eye-catching heavy-weight; the gangly detective, in the blue corner, was the unspectacular puny-weight. My money was on the gorilla, but this turned out to be a stupid selection because the great detective flashed his eyes at Mrs. Hudson, indicating that she should hold off from a truncheon attack, and suddenly threw a right hook of vicious power and speed. His fist landed perfectly upon the doctor's beaky nose with a sickening crack. Dr. Boycott was lifted off his feet, a look of astonishment written all over his face, and then down he came to Earth, stumbling upon the floor and then crumpling.

'My hero!' shouted Mrs. Hudson, her voice laden with sarcasm. 'Mr. Holmes – where did you learn to fight like a dirty rascal?

Oh, how we laughed!

'I say, Holmes, that was truly remarkable!' exclaimed I. 'I never knew that you had it in you.'

But Sherlock Holmes did not celebrate his easy victory. He bent over, picked up the steel poker, took it over to show Dr. Boycott, and, with a sudden effort, he straightened it out again! I gave him some warm applause and he responded with a small bow. Mrs. Hudson joined me, and then we laughed again, this time at the gorilla.

Dr. Boycott pulled himself up onto his feet, sweating profusely and smudging the blood from his leaky beak with his great big mitt. He glared at us, bellowed like the town bull, swung around and strode out of the room. We listened hard as he stumbled down the stairs, protesting all the way. When we heard the front door slam shut, Mrs. Hudson said: 'You are full of surprises, Mr. Holmes.'

'I was trained in the noble art by one of the great boxing champions. I learned that he was a strange man who had a penchant for the boys. The best way to avoid his advances was by standing up to him. It was the focus of my incentive and I was entirely successful in that objective.'

'I'll wager that it was, Holmes!' said I.

'Hear, hear!' quipped Mrs. Hudson and departed. Holmes turned to look at me.

'Dr. Boycott seems a very amiable person,' said he, laughing. 'I am not quite so bulky, but if he had been stubborn I might have shown him a lesson in boxing.'

'Holmes, I have never witnessed you in a boxing bout.'

'The only opportunity that we have had together, dear Doctor, was when we were caught up in the Queen's Inn last Christmas, on that wild goose chase. I seem to remember you did not fancy my chances against the doorman there, *Le Grenouille de Guadeloupe*, am I not right?'*

'He is the ex-middleweight champion of the civilised world, Holmes.'

'That chap Boycott certainly was not. But how rude of him to walk in here, unannounced, and to confound me with the official detective force! His insolence, however, gives zest to our investigation and I only trust that our new client will not suffer from her imprudence in allowing this brute to trace her. And now, Watson, I shall walk down to Doctors' Commons, where I hope to get some data which may help us in this matter. After that, we shall travel to Surrey when you will tell me what designs you have upon my sister.'

---

* see *A Gander at the Blue Carbuncle*

Well, her fellatio wasn't much to write home about, so there was a design for improvement there, but otherwise there wouldn't be much for me to say.

* * *

It was nearly twelve o'clock when Sherlock Holmes returned from his excursion. He held in his hand a sheet of paper, scrawled over with notes and figures.

'I have seen the will of the deceased wife,' said he. 'To determine its exact meaning, I have been obliged to work out the present prices of the investments with which it is concerned. The total income, which at the time of the wife's death was little short of £1,100, is now, through the fall in agricultural prices, not more than £750. Each daughter can claim an income of £250, in case of marriage. It is evident, therefore, that if both girls had married this beauty, Boycott, would have had a mere pittance, while even one of them would cripple him to a serious extent. My morning's work has not been wasted, since it has proved that he has the very strongest of motives for standing in the way of any marriage. And now, Watson, this is too serious for dawdling, especially as the old man is aware that we are interesting ourselves in his affairs, so if you are ready we shall catch a cab and drive to Waterloo railway station. I should be very much obliged if you would slip your revolver into your pocket. A Henry Holland Boxer .577 is an excellent argument with a gentleman who can twist steel pokers into knots.'

'With the Manstopper in one one's hand it is a one-sided argument for sure,' said I, with a smile, whilst ambling over to the Napoleon escritoire.

'That and a tooth-brush are, I think, all that we need.'

'This, and a tooth-brush *each* is all that we need, my friend.' I opened the draw and marvelled at the beauty of this powerful revolver, its engraved body gleaming silver in the sunshine before I gripped it in my hand and carried it off. It was too bulky for a coat pocket, so I decided that I would transport it in my medical bag – that, too, might be useful if Holmes found himself in an actual boxing match with Dr. Boycott, who I fancied to be the likely winner in a bout against the great detective, such was his size and weight advantage. One punch from the irascible Boycott could send the spindly detective into next week. Ha! That would be a fine revenge for making fun of my hangover.

At Waterloo we were fortunate in catching a train for Leatherhead, where we hired a trap at the station inn, and drove for four or five miles through the lovely Surrey lanes. It was a perfect day, with a bright sun and a few fleecy clouds scooting across the heavens, and I was fully recovered from the hangover, feeling quite chipper, actually. Oh, the joy of being in the Spring countryside! The trees and wayside hedges just throwing out their first green shoots, the air full of the pleasant scents and smells of the moist earth filling my nostrils. To me at least there was a strange contrast between the sweet promise of the Spring and this sinister quest upon which we were engaged. My companion sat in front of the trap, his arms folded, his hat pulled down over his eyes, and his chin sunk upon his breast, buried in the deepest thought. Suddenly, however, he started. He tapped me on the shoulder and pointed over the meadows.

'Look there,' said he.

A heavily timbered park stretched up in a gentle slope, thickening into a grove at the highest point.

From amidst the branches there jutted out the grey gables and rooftree of a very old mansion.

'Stoke Moran?' enquired Sherlock Holmes.

'Yes, sir, that be the house of Dr. Grimesby Boycott,' remarked the driver, who was, as usual, a be-whiskered yokel who spoke in rural drawl. Why were all the drivers in our adventures and outside London Town be-whiskered yokels? And why did they talk in a brogue that was commonplace in Devon but never in Surrey?

'There is some building going on there,' said Holmes. 'That is where we are going.'

'There be the village, sorr!' said the yokel.

'Hold on,' said I, all formal-like; 'why are you saying "there *be* the village?"'

He turned his head and gave me a clever grin. '*Whoy, thank you, sir!*' exclaimed the bumpkin, now speaking with an exaggerated and sarcastic burr. 'Oi nearly forgot my place, I did, *my old shag*. So...let me see...'. He pointed to building works on the house. 'There *be* the village, but if you *wants* to *gets* to the house, you'll find a short-cut *yonder*, by a mile, over that stile, and *oi'm* a poet, don't-yer-knowit? *Thence by yon* footpath o'er *them thar* fields. There it be! Where *yon* lady is walking.'

The faux-rustic beamed at both of us, absolutely thrilled to the quick with his rendition.

'Head up, Watson! Can't you see that lady over there is Miss Stoner?' observed the great detective, shading his eyes.

'Sharona?'

'Yes, it is Sharona. I think we had better do as our driver suggests.'

We got off the trap, I paid the fare (as usual), plus tip (as always), and the yokel rattled his way off, back towards Leatherhead, no doubt laughing all the way to the pub to tell his friends how he had fooled and fleeced some London visitors.

'I thought it as well,' said Holmes, as we climbed the stile, 'that this fellow should think we had come here as architects, on some definite business.'

I stopped. I stared at him long and hard. 'Why, on Earth, Holmes, would that yokel think that we are architects? I am dressed like a rural physician – I even carry a medical bag with me – and then there is you, all la-di-da in your morning coat, silk topper and swordstick, looking like you own the county! He may act all cider-country, but I can assure you, he is as clever as a hawk.'

'Well, when you put it like that, Doctor, maybe I was deluding myself... a little.'

We were intercepted by our client.

'Good afternoon, Miss Stoner. You see that we have been as good as our word.'

Our client of the morning had hurried forward to meet us with a face which spoke her joy. 'I have been waiting so eagerly for you,' she cried, shaking hands with us warmly. 'All has turned out splendidly. Dr. Boycott has gone to town, and it is unlikely that he will be back before evening.'

'We have had the pleasure of making the Doctor's acquaintance,' said Holmes, and in a few words he sketched out what had occurred. Miss Stoner turned white to the lips as she listened.

'Good heavens!' she cried. 'He has followed me, then.'

'So it appears.'

'He is so cunning that I never know when I am safe from him. What will he say when he returns?'

'He must guard himself, for he may find that there is someone more cunning than himself upon his track. You must lock yourself away from him tonight. If he is violent, we shall take you away to the Hudsons, my friends who live nearby. Now, we must make the best use of our time, so kindly take us at once to the rooms which we are to examine.'

The building was of grey, lichen-blotched stone, with a high central portion, and two curving wings, like the claws of a crab, thrown out on each side. In one of these wings the windows were broken, and blocked with wooden boards, while the roof was partly caved in; a picture of ruin. The central portion was in a little better repair, but the right-hand block was comparatively modern, and the blinds in the windows, with the blue smoke curling up from the chimneys, showed that this was where the family resided. Some scaffolding had been erected against the end wall, and the stonework had been broken into, but there were no signs of any workmen at the moment of our visit. Holmes walked slowly up and down the ill-trimmed lawn and examined with deep attention the outsides of the windows.

'This, I take it, belongs to the room in which you used to sleep, the centre one to your sister's. and the one next to the main building to Dr. Boycott's chamber?'

'Exactly so. But I am now sleeping in the middle one.'

'Pending the alterations, as I understand. By the way, there does not seem to be any very pressing need for repairs at that end wall.'

'There were none. I believe that it was an excuse to move me from my room.'

'Ah! That is suggestive. Now, on the other side of this narrow wing runs the corridor from which these three rooms open. There are windows in it, of course?'

'Yes, but very small ones. Too narrow for anyone to pass through.'

'As you both locked your doors at night, your rooms were unapproachable from that side. Now, would you have the kindness to go into your room, and to bar your shutters.'

Miss Stoner did so, and Holmes, after a careful examination through the open window, endeavoured in every way to force the shutter open, but without success. There was no slit through which a knife could be passed to raise the bar. Then, with his lens he tested the hinges, but they were of solid iron, built firmly into the massive masonry. 'Hmmm!' said he, scratching his chin in some perplexity, 'my theory certainly presents some difficulties. No one could pass these shutters if they were bolted. Well, we shall see if the inside throws any light upon the matter.'

A small side-door led into the whitewashed corridor from which the three bedrooms opened. Holmes refused to examine the third chamber, so we passed at once to the second, that in which Miss Stoner was now sleeping, and in which her sister had met her fate. It was a homely little room, with a low ceiling and a gaping fireplace, after the fashion of old country houses. A brown chest of drawers stood in one corner, a narrow white-counterpaned bed in another, and a dressing-table on the left-hand side of the window. These articles, with two small wicker-work chairs, made up all the furniture in the room, save for a square of Wilton carpet in the centre. The boards round and the panelling of the walls were brown, worm-eaten oak, so old and discoloured that it may have dated from the original building of the house. Holmes drew one of the chairs into a corner. I leaned against a mahogany tallboy and Miss Stoner planted her peachy on the edge of the bed. All three of us had a full view of the room; Holmes sat silent, while his eyes travelled round and round and up and down, taking in every detail.

'Where does that bell communicate with?' he asked at last, pointing to a thick bell-rope which hung down beside the bed, the tassel actually lying upon the pillow.

'It goes to the housekeeper's room.'

'It looks newer than other things.'

'Yes, it was only put there a couple of years ago.'

'Your sister asked for it, I suppose?'

'No, I never heard her using it. We used always to get what we wanted for ourselves.'

'Indeed, it seemed unnecessary to put so nice a bell-pull there. You will excuse me for a few minutes while I satisfy myself as to this floor.' He threw himself down upon his face with his lens in his hand, and crawled swiftly backwards and forwards, examining minutely the cracks between the boards. Then he did the same with the woodwork with which the chamber was panelled. Finally, he walked over to the bed and spent some time in staring at it, and in running his eye up and down the wall. Eventually, and more finally, he took the bell-rope in his hand and gave it a brisk tug.

'Why. It's a dummy.'

'Won't it ring?'

'No, it is not even attached to a wire. This is very interesting. You can see now that is fastened to a hook just above where the little opening of the ventilator is.'

'How very absurd! I never noticed that before.'

'Very strange!' muttered Holmes, pulling at the rope. 'There are one or two very singular points about this room. For example, what a fool a builder must be to open a ventilator in another room, when, with the same trouble, he might have communicated with the outside air!'

'That is also quite modern,' said the lady.

'Done about the same time as the bell-rope,' remarked Holmes.

'Yes, there were several little changes carried out about that time.'

'They seem to have been of most interesting character – dummy bell-ropes, and ventilators which do not ventilate.'

'Cowboy builders, Holmes!'

'Shut up, Watson. Now, with your permission, Miss Stoner, we shall now carry our researches into the inner apartment.'

Holmes stood up from his chair and stretched out his arm in entreaty for Miss Stoner to depart. She passed me by, still propping up the tallboy. After the put-down that my companion had given me, she lobbed me a look that belittled my good-standing as she left the room. It was hardly my fault that I was full of the joys of Spring! I was feeling so much better than I had in the morning, and I was trying to lift the mood a tad. Holmes walked forward to join me and I raised a smile whilst opening the nearest drawer, purely out of curiosity. A cloud of feminine scent wafted up. Both of us peered inside. We studied rows of neatly-displayed underwear – Miss Stoner's underwear! There were slips, girdles, brassieres, corsets and a host of ladies' grollies. As you may recall, dear adventure-enthusiast, I am somewhat an admirer of lingerie, always seeking new material – no pun intended – to add to my files of knowledge, and there, in front my eyes, were many varieties of the most conservative designs I had ever seen. Still, regardless of their sobriety, did they pass the test?

'Come along, Watson!' hissed the great detective, as he ripped off the lacey muff-smugglers from my head. 'This is a most fascinating case and I don't wish to lose it due to one of your fetishes!'

We joined Miss Stoner outside Dr. Grimsesby Boycott's chamber as she fought the handle to gain entry. 'The devil! He has locked it and taken the key with him.' She dropped her arms in defeat and dropped a moose face. Holmes and I smiled cunningly at one other, which she noticed. 'What is so amusing, gentlemen? This does not defeat you?' she enquired.

'This type of obstruction, Miss Stoner,' I beamed to her, whilst Holmes rummaged around in his coat pocket for his tools of the trade, 'is a natural obstacle to detectives. Mister Holmes will deal with it, off pat.' Holmes produced triumphantly a set of slim metal prongs on a ring, all notched at different levels. 'My dear friend, is it a multi chamber security?'

Oh! How I adore the smell of fresh lingerie!

'For goodness sakes, Watson, please do not fret,' said he, as he knelt down by the door and inserted his tool into the aperture. 'It is a common-or-garden, day-to-day sneck.'

Miss Stoner and I stood back and admired his expert fingers working the picks. With a grunt, a muffled curse and a double-click, the door swung open. We were in! For the first time during this adventure, our client's face lit up. She smiled.

'That is a most useful skill, Mister Holmes. Once this matter is settled, I shall have a small favour to ask of you, one that is of a highly personal nature.'

'You may ask any favour of me and it will be my pleasure,' greased Holmes, taking her hand and slobbering all over it whilst peaking his eyebrows towards me. Then, he turned and led the way into the chamber.

The room was larger than that of his stepdaughter but was as plainly furnished. A camp-bed, a small wooden shelf full of books, mostly of a technical character, an armchair beside the bed, a plain wooden chair against the wall, a round table, and a large iron safe were the principal things which met the eye. Holmes walked slowly round and examined each and all of them with the keenest interest.

'What is in here?' he asked, tapping the safe.

'My stepfather's business papers.'

'Oh! You have seen inside, then?'

'Only once, some years ago. I remember that it was full of papers.'

'There isn't a cat in it, for example?'

'Shut up, Watson!'

'Your companion really does have a beguiling imagination, Mr. Holmes!'

'Ignore him, Miss Stoner.'

'Excuse me, ladies and gentlemen, but look at this!' I took up a small saucer of milk which stood on the top of the safe.

'Ah! I see what you mean, Doctor. My criticism of you was premature and ill-judged.'

'No, no, Miss Stoner...' Holmes chipped in. 'Do not mollify or indulge him.'

'Oh yes I shall, Mr. Holmes! My apologies to you, Doctor. In answer to your original query: no, we do not keep a cat. But there is a cheetah and a baboon.'

'Ah, yes, of course! I remember you telling us. Well, fortunately, Miss Stoner, my companion here is an expert at catching cheetahs.'

'Thank you, Doctor, you make me feel awkward, but it is true; I am! And, obviously, the saucer of milk does not go very far in satisfying the needs of a cheetah. Miss Stoner – there is one point which I should wish to determine.' He squatted down in front of the wooden chair and examined the seat of it with the greatest attention.

'Good! That is quite settled,' said he, rising and putting his lens in his pocket. 'Hello! Here I see something interesting!'

The object which had caught his eye was a small dog leash hung on one corner of the bed. The leash, however, was curled upon itself, and tied so as to make a loop of whipcord.

'What do you make of that, Watson?'

'It is a common enough dog leash. But I don't know why it should be tied.'

'That is not quite so common, is it? Ah, it is all falling into place!' he announced. Then, his face dropped a few feet. 'This is a wicked world that we live in, and when a clever man turns his brain to crime it is the worst of all. I think that I have seen enough now, Miss Stoner, and, with your permission, we shall walk out upon the lawn.'

I had never seen my friend's face so grim, or his brow so dark, as it was when we turned from the scene of this investigation. We had walked several times up and down the lawn, neither Miss Stoner nor myself liking to break in upon his thoughts before he roused himself from his reverie.

'It is very essential, Miss Stoner,' said he, 'that from now on you should absolutely follow my advice in every respect.'

'I shall most certainly do so.'

'The matter is too serious for any hesitation. Your life may depend upon your compliance.'

'I assure you that I am in your hands.'

'In the first place, both my friend and I must spend the night in your room.'

Both Miss Stoner and I stared at him in astonishment. Suddenly, for the first time since I had scotched it from my memory, I had a flashback to the last time I was in a bedroom with Holmes and a young lady, to a case of only last year when the mysterious disappearance of Mr. Neville St. Clair took us to his house in Kent. I had experienced the most terrifying dream of my life; a nightmare that I had never shared with Sherlock Holmes but he knew every detail about it! *Every* detail! And still, to this day, I am haunted by the images of the two of us and Mrs. St. Claire in a *ménage à trois*. It is recalled in such vivid detail that I cannot be sure whether it was a dream... or reality.*

'Yes, it must be so, but you will not be with us, so do not worry yourself. Let me explain. I believe that is the village inn over there?'

'Over those two fields divided by the wire fence, one of which is a bottomless boggy marsh, over the running stream without a bridge? Yes, that is the Crown Inn.'

'Very good. Your windows would be visible from there?'

'Certainly, but only if you possess a very powerful pair of field glasses.'

'We shall find some, won't you, Doctor?'

'Yes, Holmes, I shall, but may I be so bold as to point out that in the other field, the one nearest to us here, has what looks like a Limousin bull living in it? If so, it is a rather aggressive breed.'

'Nonsense, Watson. That is a Hereford. Now, Miss Stoner, you must confine yourself to your room, on pretence of a headache maybe to your stepfather, when he comes back. Then, when you hear him retire for the night, you must open the shutters of your window, undo the hasp, put your lamp there as a signal to us, and then withdraw with everything which you are likely to want in the room which you used to occupy. I have no doubt that, in spite of the repairs, you could manage there for one night.'

---

* see *The Man with the Hairy Face*

'Oh, yes, easily.'

'The rest you will leave in our hands.'

'But what will you do?'

'Once we view your lamp in the window, we shall make our way here by crossing those two fields, the ones divided by the wire fence. We shall find our way through the bottomless marsh, swim over the running stream without a bridge, run faster than the bull in the field closest to us here and then spend the night in your room. Thus, we shall investigate the cause of this noise which has disturbed you.'

'I believe, Mr. Holmes,' said Miss Stoner, laying her hand upon my companion's sleeve, 'that you and Dr. Watson will either succeed in your mission or you will die valiantly in trying achieve it.'

Did she say "die?"

'I think that you have already made up your mind.'

'Perhaps I have.'

'Then for pity's sake, can you not tell me what was the cause of my sister's death?'

'I should prefer to have clearer proofs before I speak.'

'You could at least tell me whether my own thought is correct, and if she died from sudden fright.'

'No, I do not think so. I think that there was probably some more tangible cause. And now, Miss Stoner, we must leave you, for if Dr. Boycott returned and saw us, our journey would be in vain. Good-bye, and be brave, for if you will do what I have told you, you may rest assured that we shall soon drive away the dangers that threaten you.'

Holmes re-locked the door with his picks. We headed off down the driveway as fast as our legs would carry us, not because we were in fear of Dr Boycott returning from London Town but in case the cheetah and the baboon were on the loose!

* * *

Sherlock Holmes and I had no difficulty engaging a bedroom and a sitting room at the Crown Inn. I asked for the use of their strongest binoculars and had the better offer of a telescope, usually hired out to stargazing guests. However, I told the landlord that we were Peeping Toms, a joke that fell flat with the somewhat humourless man.

Our rooms were on the upper floor, and from our window we could command a view of the avenue gate, and of the inhabited wing of Stoke Moran Manor House. At dusk, we saw Dr. Grimesby Boycott drive past, his huge form looming up beside the little figure of the lad who drove him. The telescope was a powerful unit, and so we could view the boy having some slight difficulty in unlocking the heavy iron gates and witness the irascible Doctor screaming with fury and shaking his clenched fists at him. The trap drove on up the driveway, and a few minutes later we saw lights spring up all over the inhabited wing. About an hour later, we noticed a light shine over the fields as the lamp handled by our client was lit in one of the sitting-rooms.

'There goes Sharona, off to the land of nod!' opined Holmes, parting company with the telescope.

'In her slinkiest underwear?' quipped I. 'Maybe that little sky blue, gauzy number?'

'I really cannot imagine, Doctor, but I know that you like to. Now, we have a little while to wait until we can make our next move. Let us sit down and chew the cud on this case.'

As we sat together in the gathering darkness, Holmes stared at me for a while. Just as I was becoming uneasy under his gaze he let me know why.

'Do you know, Watson, I have really some scruples about taking you along tonight. There is a distinct element of danger.'

'Can I be of assistance?'

'Your presence might be invaluable.'

'And what about this?' I extracted the Boxer revolver from my medical bag and brandished it in the candlelight.

'Yes, even the Manstopper may be useful.'

'Then I shall certainly come.'

'It is very kind of you.'

'You speak of danger. You have evidently seen more in these rooms than was visible to me.'

'No, we have both seen the same but I fancy that I may have deduced a little more. I imagine you know that already, me being a detective and all that.'

'I noticed nothing remarkable save the saucer of milk.'

'What about the bell-rope?'

Oh, yes, that too. What purpose that serves I confess is more than I can imagine.'

'You saw the ventilator too?'

'Yes, but I do not think that is such a very unusual thing to have a small opening between two rooms. It was so small that a rat could hardly pass through.'

'I knew that we should find a ventilator before ever we came to Stoke Moran.'

'Oh, my dear Holmes, really, 'scuse my French, but what a load of bollocks!'

'Well, I tell you, Doctor, oh yes I did! You remember in Miss Stoner's statement she said that her sister could smell Dr. Boycott's cigar?'

'Er, I don't remember every detail from this morning, Holmes...'

'Indeed, you surpassed yourself, Doctor, especially when one considers that yesterday we turned in early yesterday evening.'

He was correct. We had found our beds early, but what he didn't know was what had occurred whilst he was sleeping: the *extra-curriculae* with Rachel which led to my one hour of sleep.

'Yes, it is indeed strange, Holmes, that I could not rest. I think it was something that I ate at luncheon.'

'Hmm, no doubt,' said he, his voice tinged with an air of suspicion (but at least he didn't give me an inquisitive stare). 'Anyway, back to Miss Stoner's statement. She said that she could smell the cigar smoke. Now, of course that suggests at once that there must be a communication between the two rooms. It could only be a small one, or it would have been remarked upon at the coroner's inquiry. I deduced: a ventilator!'

I threw my hands together and clapped. He smiled and inclined his head in false modesty, the vain creature, eventually putting up his hands to stop my applause.

'Bravo! But tell me, Holmes, what harm can there be in having the ventilator?'

'Well, there is a curious coincidence of dates. A ventilator is made, a cord is hung, and a lady who sleeps in the bed dies. Does that not strike you?'

'I cannot see any connection.'

'Did you observe anything very peculiar about that bed?'

'No.'

'It was clamped to the floor. Did you ever see a bed fastened like that before?'

'I cannot say that I have...Oh! Hold on, though... Yes! The Billericay Beauties have their bed clamped to the floor. And, actually, bolted to the wall adjacent.'*

'I believe you, Watson, but they would need that for the singular purpose of restraint. In this instance, it was clamped so the lady could not move her bed. It would always be in the same relative position to the ventilator and to the rope – for so we may call it – since it was clearly never designed to be a bell-pull.'

'Holmes!' I cried, 'I seem to see dimly what you are hinting at. We are only just in time to prevent some subtle and horrible crime.'

'Subtle enough and horrible enough. When a doctor does go wrong he is the finest of criminals.'

'There is hope for me yet, then?'

He ignored me. 'Dr. Boycott has nerve and he has knowledge. Palmer and Pritchard were among the heads

---

* see *The Oranges of Death!*

of their profession. This man strikes even deeper, but I think, Watson, that we shall be able to strike deeper still. But we shall have horrors enough before the night is over; we have a few hours yet, for goodness sake, so let us have a quiet pipe, and maybe some...' He shot me a glance that guided my eyes over to my medical bag, which was still open. 'And maybe another visit to the phial of the pure stuff which you have in there? We didn't quite finish it off this morning, and it, er, may go off, er... like your luncheon of yesterday?'

'All right, Holmes, you win. I shall only allow it on the grounds of your imminent danger. Tonight, you need to boldly go where no man has ever been before.'

'Inside Sharona's underwear?'

We both laughed so hard that we crashed out of our chairs!

* * *

About nine o'clock the light among the trees was extinguished, and all was dark across the two fields in the direction of the Manor House. Two hours passed slowly away, and then, suddenly, just at the stroke of eleven, a single bright light shone out right in front of us.

'That is our signal,' said Holmes. He seemed much brighter than earlier on. Mind you, he should have been, having finished off the phial of cocaine. The drug would also make him obtuse and playful. Ho hum!

As we passed out of the front door of the Crown Inn, he exchanged a few words with the landlord, explaining that we were going on a late visit to an acquaintance, and, that it was possible that we might spend the night there. The landlord raised his eyebrows at Holmes's stream of words delivered at an unusually high speed.

Then, he enquired of us as to why we would pay for the rooms when we were not going to sleep in them, to which Holmes replied: "Ha, that we should be so lucky!" As there was no sensible answer, a moment later we were out on the dark road. A chill wind was blowing in our faces, and one yellow light was twinkling in front of us across the fields to guide us on our sombre errand. Just as I was climbing over the fence to gain access to the first field, I noticed that Sherlock Holmes was starting to walk away, down the road towards the front gates of Stoke Moran Manor House. I stopped.

'This way, Holmes!' I shouted. He stopped and glanced over his shoulder. 'Did you not say that it would be most unwise for us to walk through the front gates and up the driveway?'

'And traipse over those two fields divided by the wire fence, the near one being a bottomless boggy marsh; then, traverse the running stream when there is no bridge; and then tackle the bull in the far field, which is probably a Limousin and, therefore, probably just as nasty as Dr. Boycott?'

'You told me that it was a Hereford!'

'Well, I may have got that wrong...'

'Oh! So, instead, we take our chances of meeting a cheetah, a baboon *and* Dr. Boycott, the gorilla of Stoke Moran?'

'Yes, I think so. If we are assaulted by either, you can shoot them with the Manstopper.'

We walked along the road through the gloom. In fact, we didn't need to use the gates or the driveway because there was little difficulty in entering the grounds, for unrepaired breaches gaped in the old park wall. Making our way among the trees, we reached the lawn, crossed it, and were about to enter through the window, when out from a clump of laurel bushes there darted what seemed to be a hideous and distorted child, who threw himself on the grass with writhing limbs, and then ran swiftly across the lawn into the darkness.

'My God,' I whispered, 'did you see that?'

Holmes was for the moment as startled as I. His hand closed like a vice upon my wrist in his agitation. Then he broke into a low laugh and put his lips to my ear.

'Stop it! That tickles!'

'Sshhh, Watson,' he murmured, 'that is the baboon!'

'He hasn't seen us, thank God. There is the cheetah, too. Perhaps we might find it upon our shoulders at any moment?'

'Cheetahs are diurnal creatures. It is more likely that it is asleep.'

We slipped off our shoes and tip-toed a pathway to the bedroom window. Soon we were inside. My companion closed the shutters, moved the lamp onto the table and cast his eyes round the room. All was as we had seen it in the daytime. Then, creeping up to me and making a trumpet of his hand, he whispered into my ear again so gently that it tingled and tickled more than before and it was all I could do to distinguish the words:

'The least sound would be fatal to our plans.'

I nodded, then pulled away quickly to scratch the itch that Holmes's breath had caused on my outer ear, on the pinna, the helix and the bulla.

He moved in again, this time even closer. 'We must sit without light. He would see it through the ventilator.'

'Get off!' I hissed, pushing him away.

He moved in again, this time his lips were right on my shell-like.

'Listen! Your very life may depend upon it.' His lips were brushing all over my helix, making me tingle in a distressingly unnatural way. 'Have your revolver ready in case we should need it. I will sit on the side of the bed, and you in that chair over there.'

I tried to pull away to get to it, but he resisted, tightening his grip on my shoulders and pulling me in close once more.

'Just one more thing...' he hissed. Suddenly his tongue darted deep into my concha! I jumped up in the air but his strong hands restrained me and I could hear him chuckle. 'Quiet, now, Doctor...' and he blew a soft stream of air onto my ear before letting me go. I took off like a greyhound and snuck into the seat of the chair. Even in the lamplit gloom I could still make him out laughing silently to himself.

I took out my revolver and laid it on the corner of the table.

Holmes brought up a long thin cane, and this he placed upon the bed beside him. Where he produced that from, goodness knows! By it he laid a box of matches and the stump of a candle. Then he turned down the lamp and we were left in darkness.

How shall I ever forget that dreadful vigil? I could not hear a sound, not even the drawing of breath, and yet I knew that my friend sat open-eyed, within a few feet of me, in the same state of nervous tension in which I was myself. The shutters cut off the least ray of light, and we waited in absolute darkness. From outside came the occasional cry of a night-bird, and once at our very window a long drawn, cat-like whine, which told us that the cheetah may have been diurnal by nature, but tonight he was out on a whoop-up with the baboon!

Far away we could hear the deep tones of the parish clock, which boomed out every quarter of an hour. How long they seemed, those quarters! Twelve o'clock, and one, and two, and three, and still we sat waiting silently for whatever might befall. I recounted my escapade with Rachel the night before. I had ventured out about nine o'clock, quiet as a mouse. We met up and spent three hours together drinking port and brandy in the dark caverns of Gordons. We left Villiers Street at about one in the morning and sneaked back into the 221B apartment. There ensued an almighty amount of hush-hush fiddling between the sheets that ended with an untimely eruption, like she had dropped a match into my box of fireworks. Sadly, nothing else happened before we passed out. Ho hum – I looked forward to the next time! At least we were fortunate that her brother never woke up, and that Rachel slept on the floor out of sight. Otherwise, this morning, he would have shaken me awake by the throat.

Suddenly there was a momentary gleam of light up in the direction of the ventilator! It vanished immediately but was succeeded by a strong smell of burning oil and heated metal. Someone in the next room had lit a dark lantern. I heard a gentle sound of movement, and then all was silent once more, though the smell grew stronger. For half an hour I sat with straining ears. Then suddenly another sound became audible – a very gentle, soothing sound, like that of a small jet of steam escaping continually from a kettle. The instant that we heard it, Holmes sprang from the bed, struck a match, and lashed furiously with his cane at the bell-pull.

'You see it, Watson?' he yelled. 'You see it?'

But I saw nothing. At the moment when Holmes struck a light I heard a low, clear whistle, but the sudden glare flashing into my eyes made it impossible for me to tell what it was at which my friend lashed so savagely. I could, however, see that his face was deadly pale, and filled with horror and loathing.

He had ceased to strike, and was gazing up at the ventilator, when suddenly there broke from the silence of the night the most horrible cry which I have ever heard. It swelled up louder and louder, a shrill yell of pain and fear and terror mingled into one dreadful shriek. They say that away down in the village, and even in the distant parsonage, that eerie wail raised the living and the dead from their beds. It struck cold into our hearts, and I stood gazing at Holmes, and he at me, until the last echoes of it had died away into the silence from which it rose.

'What can that mean?' I gasped.

'It means that it is all over,' Holmes answered. 'And perhaps, after all, it is for the best. Take your revolver, and we shall enter Dr. Boycott's room.'

With a grave face he lit the lamp and led the way down the corridor. Twice he knocked on the chamber door without any reply from within. Then he turned the handle and it stayed put. It was locked. He knelt down and squinted through the keyhole.

Watching Holmes that night reminded me of school, the happiest days of my life!

'Drat! He has locked it from the inside and left the key in situ.'

Using his pickers Holmes wrestled with the lock. A few moments later we could hear the key drop onto the floorboards inside the room. Holmes made a fresh assault launched upon the tumblers and a few seconds later we entered, with me at his heels and the cocked Manstopper in my hand.

It was a singular sight which met our eyes. On the table stood a dark lantern with the shutter half open, throwing a brilliant beam of light upon the iron safe, the door of which was ajar. Beside this table, on the wooden chair, sat Dr. Grimesby Boycott, clad in his long grey dressing-gown, his bare ankles protruding beneath, and his feet thrust into red heel-less Turkish slippers. Across his lap lay the short stock with the long lash which we had noticed during the day. His chin was cocked upwards, and his eyes were fixed in a dreadful stare at the corner of the ceiling. Round his brow he had a peculiar yellow band, with brownish speckles, which seemed to be bound tightly round his head. As we entered he made neither sound nor motion.

'The band! The speckled band!' whispered Holmes.

I took a step forward. In an instant his strange headgear began to move, and there reared itself from among his hair the squat diamond-shaped head and puffed neck of a loathsome serpent.

'I say, Holmes, is that not a snake?'

'It is a swamp adder!' cried Holmes. 'The deadliest snake in India!'

Snakes did not agree with me. I took a couple of steps backwards.

'Boycott has brought it here and he has died within ten seconds of being bitten. We must capture this creature and put it back into its den, and then we can remove Miss Stoner to some place of shelter and let the county police know what has happened.'

That was Sherlock Holmes! Practical and methodical, even in the presence of a killer snake. He drew the dog whip swiftly from the dead man's lap but before he could wield it against the snake I stepped forwards and shoved him to one side. I was taking no chances whatsoever with Mr. Swamp Adder!

'I have this under control, my friend…' said I, raising the Manstopper into position, clasping the grip tightly with both hands and lining up the barrel sight with the vile, ugly, grinning snake. As I took aim the serpent sensed danger. It reared up even higher and let out a nerve-rattling hiss. Its evil eyes mesmerised me. I had to be rid of it! I squeezed the golden trigger. There was an instantaneous flash of orange light followed by a mind-boggling explosion of unbelievable magnitude! From that moment on, I am not sure precisely what happened. I have an everlasting vision, like a recurring nightmare, of Holmes staggering backwards and opening his mouth slowly, ever so slowly, as if he was at the start of an ejaculation, but with no sound. I never heard his voice. Nor did I hear another thing in this world for another twenty-four hours as the .577 Holland Boxer leapt into life. It was like Mount Vesuvius erupting in my hands! A searing pain coursed through my veins and exploded in my wrists. Then, I was thrown upwards, into a sensation of weightlessness, flying through the air upside down and backwards, taking in a tremendous view of the ceiling – and wondering when the decorator would be in – before landing on my backside in the hallway outside the room. My senses were shattered, all apart from taste, which suddenly sprang to the front of my mouth, the most extraordinary metallic flavour biting my tongue, as if I had been eating a tin can.

When I sat up and looked back into the room, the swamp adder was gone. So was Dr. Boycott's head. I had scored a direct hit with the Manstopper!

* * *

Such are the true facts of the death of Dr. Grimesby Boycott, of Stoke Moran, what was left of him. I won't prolong the narrative, which has already run too great a length, by telling how we broke the sad news to the terrified Sharona, how we conveyed her to the fine home of Paul and Henya Hudson, in the nearby village of Fetcham. It was there, that evening, that Miss Stoner had recovered sufficiently for her to ask that special favour from the great detective, the one which she had alluded to the day before. Sherlock Holmes ingratiated his client immediately. He heaved her up onto the fine oak kitchen table there and then, and went to work on her chastity belt – the one that her stepfather had attached to her and we couldn't find the key – whilst our host mined the cocktail cabinet for joyful concoctions. After that minor inconvenience, she was a very different person, as if the belt had been manacles. Her face lit up; she smiled; she laughed. She was the life and soul of the dinner party thrown that evening, not that I could hear a word that anyone said.

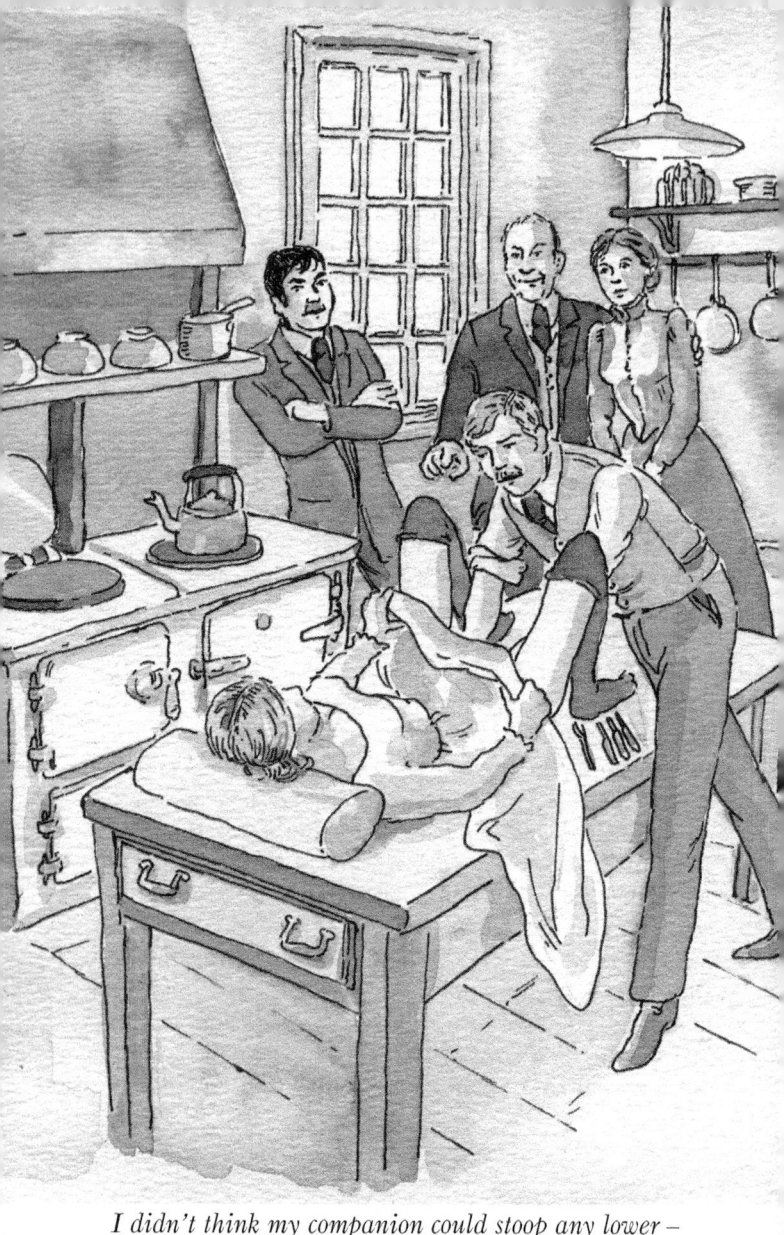

*I didn't think my companion could stoop any lower –
but then, he did!*

The slow process of official inquiry came to the conclusion that the Doctor had met his fate while indiscreetly playing with a dangerous pet – not a venomous snake, but we convinced the coroner that the baboon had ripped off its owner's head and the cheetah had eaten it. Holmes dealt with the statement of facts immediately after the event, yours truly being completely deaf, and the local plods believed every word that he told them, such was the spread of his professional reputation in *The Strand* magazine and his burgeoning influence within the Establishment. The great detective was temporarily hard of hearing himself, the explosion of the Manstopper in such a confined space being a deafening shock to the inner ears causing temporary sensorineural damage, but after a good night's rest we had recovered adequately to be able to converse when we travelled back by railway the next day.

'I had,' said he, 'come to an entirely erroneous conclusion…'

'Pardon?'

'I said, I had come to an erroneous…'

'What did you say? SPEAK UP!' But then I started to laugh, letting my mask slip, and the penny dropped.

'Shut up, Watson, and open your ears. I am trying to tell you how dangerous it always is to reason from insufficient data.'

What he was doing trying to do, in fact, dear reader, was brag about his sheer brilliance. I was now the focus of his attention for the epilogue. I was locked into a first-class compartment and had nowhere to go.

'In this case,' continued he, unabated, 'the presence of the gipsies, and the use of the word "band," which was used by the poor girl, no doubt to explain the appearance which she had caught a horrid glimpse of by the dim light of her match, were persuasive enough to put me upon an entirely wrong scent. I can only claim the merit that I instantly reconsidered my position when, however, it became clear to me that whatever danger threatened an occupant of the room could not come from either the window or the door. My attention was speedily drawn, as I have already remarked to you, to this ventilator, and to the bell-rope which hung down to the bed. The discovery that this was a dummy, and that the bed was clamped to the floor, instantly gave rise to the suspicion that the rope was there as a bridge for something passing through the hole and coming to the bed. The idea of a snake instantly occurred to me, and when I coupled it with my knowledge that the Doctor was furnished with a supply of creatures from India, I felt that I was probably on the right track. The idea of using a form of poison which could not possibly be discovered by any chemical test was just such a one as would occur to a clever and ruthless man who had an Eastern training. The rapidity with which such a poison would take effect would also, from his point of view, be an advantage. It would be a sharp-eyed coroner indeed who could distinguish the two little dark punctures which would show where the poison fangs had done their work. Then I thought of the whistle. Of course, he must recall the snake before the morning light revealed it to the victim. He had trained it, probably by the use of the milk which we saw, to return to him when summoned. He would put it through the ventilator at the hour that he thought best, with the certainty that it would crawl down the rope, and land on the bed. It might or might not bite the occupant, perhaps she might escape every night for a week, but sooner or later she must fall victim.'

Blimey, quite a post-mortem!

'I came to these conclusions before ever I had entered his room. An inspection of his chair showed me that he had been in the habit of standing on it, which, of course, would be necessary in order that he should reach the ventilator. The sight of the safe, the saucer of milk, and the loop of the whipcord were enough to dispel any doubts which may have remained. The metallic clang heard by Miss Stoner was obviously caused by her stepfather hastily closing the door of his safe which I took to prove my theories. I heard the creature hiss, as I have no doubt that you did also, and I instantly lit the light and attacked it.'

'With the result of hissing off back through the ventilator!'

'Ha! And, yes it was so *hissed off* that it turned upon its master at the other side. Some of the blows of my cane came home, and roused it into a raging temper, so that it flew upon the first person it saw; that was Dr. Boycott. In this way I am no doubt indirectly responsible for his death, and I cannot say that it is likely to weigh very heavily upon my conscience.'

'Don't worry, Holmes, if he wasn't quite dead, the Manstopper finished him off!'

'Indeed, Watson! Your revolver certainly did the trick. Now, I have a treat for you...'

The great detective's face radiated a warm, friendly, sunny smile as he leaned into his suitcase and withdrew another; the one that contained Horatio.

'Let me entertain you for the next hour or so!' And he swung the violin up to his chin. Horatio now has perfect tone.'

Maybe I was bored? Maybe my hearing had been damaged permanently? Maybe I was just 'in the mood' but what Holmes played to me was astoundingly pleasant – a medley of Russian ballads and peasant dances that ranged from simple melodies to complex movements, all of them rich in texture, full of fabric and played with passion. I asked myself: was there anything that this remarkable human being could fail to accomplish, should he decide to turn his hand?